HEKATE

HEKATE

Leila Lees

Published by 99% Press,
an imprint of Lasavia Publishing Ltd.
Auckland, New Zealand
www.lasaviapublishing.com

ISBN: 978-1-991083-21-0

for Mike Johnson
love and the poetry in us

1 open

Hekate

with tender focus
through crafting and the action of creating
I partake in the concept of ensouling

ensouling something is to bring meaning
the artistry is in the fluid connection with the material
we create from

we may ensoul things by being who we are
taking time to notice
the details, the gesture of another thing

in the Chaldean Oracles
Hekate's celestial role was to ensoul the universe
soul was woven throughout
and tightly bound to the physical world

Hekate knows the darkness that we must enter
she is there where roads cross
she is the light and the dark

Hekate is in the commencement and in the ending
she is the familiar of the liminal spaces
we travel through
she is conversant with the shapes of separation
the wick of loneliness
the lost in the limen

the limen is detached from its surroundings
here
the threshold is neither inside nor outside of the house

I cross through the liminal spaces
Hekate is in front of and behind.

beginning

a small glimmer of awakening
and I desire to cling to sleep again
I begin before I begin
I begin in the dream and when I am sleep-walking life

that's how I find myself in the labyrinth
I wake up there already walking

pūriri

I get drawn outside
by the pūriri moth's mute banging
against the artificial light
I behold its crumbling body
its striking green patterning

turning off the light I gently coax it onto my hand
and holding it carefully
I enter into the bush beside the house

I am held up
by its weight-full fragility

I sit by a young pūriri tree
I nestle in the shadows
I feel the moth rest on my hand

we are odd companions in the night

here is a heart that is void, sleepless and open
embedded in land

a heart that dreams
and mingles our edges

I lose my discernment of our dichotomy

the moth has space and it gives space
the space to stretch within

I encounter our difference
through tonal patterns in the dark

the ancestors become unruly
the land insistent

and then I get walking
I walk in the darkness beside the road

2 in darkness

heron

in darkness
the memory of the light rests inside form

I walk in the intervening space beside the path

from the shadows arise luminous weightless thinking
a creative rift of thoughts that drift into open space

the landscape shifts in a seamless manner

I let slip the desire for a settled comprehension

I arrive at a beach where the tide goes a long way out
creating mudflats, cockle beds
a place for flounder to lie in the shallow warm water

I stop

in the vestige of night, a white-throated heron listens
with elongated focus
a solitary existence within a limitless world
separateness and connection in concert

the heron moves with undisturbed reclusion
nonchalant around the presence of others

as it weaves its existence through a world
of chattering groups

the full tide laps the beach like a heartbeat
rhythmic and soft

when I move again
my feet crunch the broken shell
emptying into the silence

the heron moves effortlessly
and yet there is a gawky vulnerability
in the way it lifts its legs or turns its head to listen

the present is dreamlike
the immediacy of memory slips backwards

I embody the heron
a listening state, a slow balancing dance
I have an acute awareness of the damp air on my skin
the shadows, the water, the click of a crab
with a comfortable discernment of timing and
whereabouts
I bend my ear into the body

the heron merges with the shadows and patterns

forest

the darkness becomes complete as I enter the forest
I look up to find my way
watching for the spaces between the branches of the trees

the silence is in the in-between
and I step into it

form becomes indistinct
darkness and infinity rush in
contrasting with my sense of self
a small glint of consciousness that prevails

the colourless night with a waning moon accentuates
the milky pūriri trunks
their hollows and wounds create an eerie expansion
an undulating movement of essential form

it grows and twists to external forces
and integral
the air moves through the cavities and dark hollows
as form is eaten away

wind, light and shadow become intimate with pūriri
branches spiral, bend and wring open
fattening, narrowing
creating hollows like entrances into caves

the trunk wrinkles
like skin falling into folds as if too big for its form

where pūriri grubs enter, kākā come down the trunks
gripping with their claws
ripping off the bark with their purpose designed beaks

I am drawn into the wildering instrument of its hollows
dark shadowy spaces
shedding tensions
that have leaked into the open spaces of my psyche

I cross thresholds forgetting the small terrors of change

my feet let go their grip on the earth
letting the breath in the interstices spring them forward

and I walk through a grove of hangehange
it exudes a sweet scent of citrus
from its wax-green flowers that protrude
from the slender brittle branches and light green leaves

I slow into its otherworldly gesture
I walk through the moon-like luminosity of its leaves

like the hanged man in the Tarot
upside down, suspended
loosening my hold on my will

gently unfurling my fingers
holding too tightly to something
and now there is nothing to grasp

I see people walking old thorough ways
like a braided river emerging through past landscapes
I am reminded of people in my life
of friendships, of companions
that I have connected with and then parted from
a fleeting observation
regret
and sadness wells up
releases

the world is timeless within its physical form

I am inquisitive of the mystery
curious of the seeming paradox of form
that becomes amorphous
made up of space and starlight, everything and nothing

within, an essence, an abiding quality
that cannot be lost or overwhelmed

shapeshift

I merge and experience something other than myself
at the same time, a constancy of my own existence
existence as eternal, and essence as existence

I am a small soft-winged silence
that weaves between the trees
I land on a branch to the right of me
and look down at me with an inscrutable stare

there I am in the doorway, a valve between dimensions
I swing open

the me slips through hangehange
into a past glimpsed in peripheral vision

of an old coastal forest
that grows undisturbed for a thousand years
the ground bristling with life, fecund with deep litter
old taraire with their slow staunch trunks,
and rātā thick in weave and height
I lay down in the past
wētā serrate their legs and scuttle through the undergrowth

the dark softens into shadow

ruru call to each other
they wake my eyes
and move across to swiftly vanish

3 light issues forth

in light there is form

light seeps in
form is brushed with twilight

my walking leans me in an arc of darkness subsiding

graduated unilluminated tones
succumb to a percolating light

tūī swing their song through the dusky air
daybreak granulates like sand

green unhurriedly materialises

the light issues through green and magenta
the blowflies wake up as if summer is here
they fly rapidly with purpose

first flush

there are pink smudges near the horizon

pink is new
vulnerable yet fearless
scent of apple blossom, wild peach
the colour of baby birds before they grow their feathers
the tip of a rose petal, a wound healing

in the rose quartz crystal
pink
is a juxtaposition of soft and sharp

stone

I turn to the west, that I may linger in shadow
the light behind me picks out the outline of form
throwing the shadows long

unquiet thoughts become accentuated
fear upheaves my mind
fear of the seen, the definition, the consequence of action
fear of involvement
to partake in beauty, to create mistakes inevitable
through the illuminated world

fear is the separation
and the connection
fear is the lost in-between place where nothing happens

fear leads to pre-empting events
to act without trust, to turn from connection
to skip the heart
to rush with indecision, fluttering distraction
to deny

illusion allows me to move
I enter through this
as Hansel and Gretel entered the gingerbread house
to see the nature of allurement

in this in-between place of contraction before expression
I desire ease, to hold something solid in my hand
a small grey oval stone, greywacke molded by sea

I pick up stones
smoothed and tumbled
shaped by cycles and rhythms
transformed remains of former life

within stone
two opposing forces
immovability and movement
connection and the forgetting

a mineral trail through time
reminding me the integral exists in the broken
seeping up
cracking into form

I remember my grandmother capturing small stones
bright ones like winking eyes in the water
she collects them in the billy
and I the child spill them on the sand, freeing them
they already miss the shadow of the marram grass

in the dream the moon nestles under blankets
creeps unbidden
quiet into the grapefruit tree

and with eyes unseeing it slides the tops of pines

I am floating on a drift of scent
of flowering cherries and sweet plum
and pine and the damp moss
the smell of mown grass
before I slip into the stream resting forbidden and forgotten
in the cool water
sucking on the peppery watercress, colliding with stone

I am a remnant star lost in stone
I give up, I fall asleep, I become sedulous in my forgetting
I am pieces of soul embedded in rock
I fall off, break up, lodge in the cracks of other rocks
resting like a sleeping story

ant

ants create existence by walking
ant walking
ant sensing the perimeter
the edge of
to register the perimeter
to register the edge

ants join up the pieces of things, like a small moving thread
from one separation to another
communicating through an unobtrusive bumping
into each other

ants create cohesion

using my hands as my antennae
I would do ant-walking
feeling a stone before I encountered it

I listened for the stories imprinted
into stones
resting, waiting, hidden

threshold

I find myself slowly
I turn towards the light

the light both blinds and reveals
my separation through physical form

I feel a contraction around my heart
that in arriving into light
I have lost the nourishing shadow

in the light I grip certainty before it slips and vacillates

perhaps it is Hekate that unravels certainty
reminding me that the soul's journey traverses
through fragmentary glimpses
fluctuating and merging definitions of form and identity

the tattered heart-shaped leaves of kawakawa
hang to the east
a caterpillar of the native moth Cleora scriptaria
riddles the leaves with holes and bites

these holes remind me of lineage
invisible portals to the people behind us
when I find their footsteps they have already walked ahead

I put my feet in their cool indent

this liminal place

a passage from one mode of life to another
becomes detached a little from its surroundings

a threshold is neither inside or outside
the crossroads are the junction of roads
yet belong to none of them
the liminal place offers a variation of options
with no reassuring certainty

crossing into the temporal world
there is a shift, a wobble in perception
light wavers and settles

in the sunlight form becomes defined, form bestows
expression and life to wisdom

kōtukutuku, New Zealand tree fuchsia
grows in the forest margins, a gesture of thresholds

the flower transitions
through blues, magentas, greens
yellow and tinges of rose
a stream of variegated colour as it buds
and is pollinated

its bloom is small and complex

from a green bud, with a splash of indigo
four sepals of the kōtukutuku open out
the sepals are green before they tinge pink
eventually shifting from a rose to magenta
four small dark purple petals
poke out between the sepals
eight stamens with blue pollen extend
surrounding a single style with a yellow stigma

its bark peels and hangs in red papery strips
that show a pale wood underneath
Its branches appear straggly, broken and disorganised

the exquisite colour and precision of the flowers
are in contrast to its rambling loose appearance
kōtukutuku's visage challenges us
to integrate visually disparate features
resolves differences with fluidity and grace

I want to remember this
in times of disjunction

I cross through
temporarily tripping
through a space

and find my way along the edge of the coastal forest

the light is intensified around the tips of branches
as they delineate their separation
I look at the stones that have been pushed up on the shore
there is space in the materiality of rock
It invites me into the room of it

through the density I slip
into the crevices, the margins and the intervals

I imagine remnants of kōtukutuku colours
fusing

tūī

the sun illuminates
the fine spider webs
the flash of tūī feathers
as it moves its position in the nīkau palm

as the light permeates there is a joyous movement
within
there is life and activity and noise
tūī levitates sounds mischievously

attendance is a language of transition

but in the crisp early morning light
sunlight calls, bold movement
the tūī opens its beak
spilling a layer of throaty calls and bell like sounds
it pushes out its chest, immune to influence, alert

tūī wakes me out of slumber
I am catapulted, joyous, sad and angry all at once

I am moving
sunlight reveals the external world

4 in the wrinkles and folds

mud

I am at the edge of the estuary
walking barefoot through mud
mangrove trees poke up their aerial roots
the mud is rich with life
crabs and worms and tiny crustaceans
the mud squelches as I press my feet into it
oozing up between my toes

my ancestors lived near estuaries and harbours
they knew the currents, the rhythm of tide
the timing for gathering food
the land adjusts their bodies
clothing them in earth and mist

the landscape is layered and transparent through time
I see the river of my childhood
sprawl through wetlands
I see my grandmother standing outside her house
the river enters through the house
that stands on the drained, rich peaty soil

I watch the house teeter and slip
into mud
flax folding around it

the mud is boiling
it plops and folds inside of itself
in the upheaval
everything is absorbed

this roiling vortex counterpoises the poetic elements

I shed the night

I come into the landscape I inhabit now
I step from the mud onto the jointed stems of Salicornia
and sit on the bank eating the succulent saline stems
cleavers and hawkbit grow amongst the grass

the tide shifts
as it recedes it pushes debris back in wave patterns
small concentric circles radiate
around the breathing holes of small crabs
a whorl underneath spinning out thread breath

there are whorls at the growth tip of the cleavers plant
these wrinkle and fold as it grows up and out
like the whorls on my fingertips created through
different layers of skin growth

cleavers travels upward, a green rush
cleaving to other plants, up, through and over
light rooted, the whole plant will lift up
if tugged gently, ready for a ride

pōhutukawa

I clamber over and under
the snaking branches of pōhutukawa
these are coastal trees, strong and sheltering
the pōhutukawa's red aerial roots antennae the space
mooring in air before growing into the sky
they fold over edges, swing into empty spaces
hang hair in dense mats

sinuous with life
they find the crests and crevices of stone and clay in cliffs
broadening, twisting they become branches

the tree
layers these branches with slow grace
allowing gravity to anchor them, blind antenna growing old

and look Ariadne's thread, a line of red
goes to the source in a labyrinthine way
with the constraint of wind and sea and heart
embodies a single drop of blood
an essence of our life and infinite life
patterned as a pathway, dynamic, permeating,
flushing life,
air and fire through form

here is love and the scent of summer to come

I am inside myself, inside of you, inside the universe,
outside the universe, within
I am suspended in fire, in air

love breaks down the boundaries of things

there is no separation between form and spirit
between form and heart
between form and love

pōhutukawa
comes from a family called Myrtaceae, the myrtle family
this family is aromatic, excreting oils
in this family are mānuka and kānuka
the gum trees of Australia, cloves and of course myrtle
these trees are cousins, all of them are shedding
whether it is leaves or branches or their bark
under these trees there is always debris

I rest under the pōhutukawa
there is an array of colours in the leaves
that move and merge
from viridian green to yellow green
to yellow and orange, vermillion, carmine
and then blend towards the earth
the burnt sienna and burnt umber
rich dark humus
in concert, the early dawn colours
slip from transparent lightness to greens and yellows

a rose cloud, a band of gold, azure
every colour has its companion
the magenta calls up the viridian
there is a suffusing of the darkness by the greening

as a breeze comes, leaves drop, shedding
they pile up on the ground
light dapples, place rests in texture

in shadow, a dissipation of energy
a slow weaning away from connection
a weariness with love
I find solace in distance, a relief in giving up
I back with disillusion, ache in the dissolution
I fold into my aloneness
I tell a lie to the fire of the flowers

in the place of despair
where the heart contracts and this small light inside
daren't touch the opalescent sky
I no longer attend to the word
I grow in the same grooves
laid down by my broken ancestors
the ones that bury their fractures in smoky guilt

I hide my tender existence
I press on the sharp point of a small chipped marble
anger loses its action

I turn my resistance towards myself
I bury myself in rooms that cannot break down
I attend to other people's gardens and neglect my own
I allow the accustomed tyranny its utterance
this is how it is, this is how it's done
this is how the world is
in secret I desire to touch the despair, to enter into it
 to succumb to decay

under the pōhutukawa life is creating
through shedding
I crawl under its leaves
I smell the scent of their natural oils
they rustle and break
I go deeper, wanting to enter the damp
the fecundity of decay
In weariness I let go, trusting the disintegration
The leaves crumble, my mouth is full of earth

and like the labyrinth, lineage brings me to origin
the paradox of a journey that goes both ways
Adriadne's red thread rises to the surface

sunlight enters obliquely

5 air

pōhuehue

the late morning light delineates
the red stems of the coastal plant pōhuehue
as it grows it climbs into and over itself
forming a resilient clump
where underneath the soil stays always a little damp.

under trees it climbs towards the light

the whole of its structure is flexible
its stems extend
to bind the air
to weave it tight

it loves the air

it opens and pockets the space
through divaricating movement

it composes
through a shifting play of opposites
connection and separation, expansion and contraction
light and shadow, rest and movement

space has substance in relationship to the lean stem

space abuts axis points, angular dissections of air

it buoys the plant upwards

we called it the bouncy stuff

I become immersed in the entangled stems
playing upon a stray path
crossroads transverse crossroads
dimensions waver in the shadow and the light

I can integrate the affinities and differences
as a pattern that connects me into my surroundings
I trust in the variable, I make choices swiftly
into the fold of stem and air
this twining summons me hither

and with a sudden grasp for comprehension
I become uncertain
I search for something tangible
I have an expectation for what hasn't shown up
it is forever over there

I cannot hold air

I think I know the way, I do not want that way
I want the line and not the space, brittle control
I hunt for explanation
I move towards delineation
fine lines silhouette through from the space behind

I deliberately close connecting riverbeds
of emotion and experience

I contract backwards
emotional shock, the disturbing experience
the trauma imbedded in culture, in family
in me

in the shadow of the contracting heart
I cannot integrate
I cannot open
to play
I segregate new culture, new ideas
I create rules and boundaries, sharp and defined

I become confined by patterns laid in the past
I forget the original purpose of these patterns
so that when purpose shifts
I still chase an old template, obsolete, empty

I hide in a shadow
that involves intricate loops of self-deception
a mosaic of appearances, disappearances
faltering steps in a peregrination of defence and smiles
with volleys of ineffectual positive thoughts

grief fiercely congests the unbounded movement
then dislodges a crucible

it endures the heat and I am touched by the beauty
in the molten colours that emerge in the sunlight
patterns are revealed as a whole
they become designs that we build upon

a mutable existence
in the leaves, the ash, and the shells of beetle wings
in the soft sand under the pōhuehue
in the decomposing, in the breaking down
a steadfast consciousness.

I fall, I go into and through
I reflect back through a mosaic
parcels of memory that shift and form patterns
a turning kaleidoscope

landscape, intimate relationships with place and people
fluctuate and evolve
time plays with me
there I was and there I am not

united in the act of observation

the small ovate leaves are in my mouth and hair
I am in the midst of it, waist deep
I am the kānuka tree
pōhuehue climbs over me
entwines my ankles, imprints its stems and leaves
uses my limbs to suspend itself in the air

eventually it pulls my limbs downwards

I grow
tree caves in the sand dunes
our leaves form a matt hedge
furrows to the wind

I bend my shape to wind
surrendering
to the external influence
my heartwood is slow and rich
I hollow out

I am in the bounds of wood and branch and bark that
lifts and flakes and falls away

I slide outside to observe

thoughts stray, slip askew from its hard wood
I lose sight of kānuka and enter into the airy space

between form

the element of air carries my thoughts
they gather up other ideas and freewheel the sky
with no particular design
I merge and emerge
through diverse gestures of physical form

the kānuka bark is layered
strips hang
before falling away
riroriro and waxeyes hop down the bark
feeding off the scale insects
cicada feed on the sap
thrumming their resonant sound in the day
wētā click in the night

sooty mould

black sooty mould covers areas of the trunk
it sparkles in galaxies as light touches it

it grows on the secretion of the kānuka scale insect
the male moults
from the feeding nymph stage to a pre-pupa stage
it has small antennae and wing buds
it burrows into crevices in the bark
forms cocoons
and emerges wings, antennae, legs, compound eyes

the adult female has no wings
she stays nymph-like
she may not fly and crawls
she winters over and lays her eggs in the spring
feeding off the sap
full of sugars and waters
more than she needs
she secretes sugary waste through wax tubes

sooty mould grows on this

I see myself with a wheelbarrow
all the pieces I have shed are in the wheelbarrow
the light reflects flashes of rainbow
on these coal-black jumbled pieces

I push memory in front of me
I cannot stop or put it down

kānuka bark shreds

the stars are in the sooty mould
the pieces of bark, everything
falls away

memory leads me through aching stars
sharp in the earth's mantle

in this stretched star-encrusted world
I walk through to rich veins of coal
memory of forest

time is spun slowly, whilst life is a quickening flame

an old woman grins
spinning with gnarly hands
she admonishes me to hold it loosely

cicada

cicada enters into the world above the earth
whilst the night is in soft transition
with powerful forelegs cicada digs its way to the surface
of the ground
and crawls up the kānuka
a peregrine excursion
at the verge of sloughing off the land's embrace
it holds fast
slowly emerging from its old casing of dark earth

I open a window for my sleeping self to emerge
aspects submerged in order to survive slip to the surface
in anticipation of summer

I have wings, lattice divisions
cells arranged in dynamic tension

the sun spreads out through the tops of the trees
saturating leaves with warmth and light
the male cicada alternately tightens
and releases clusters of muscles
creating a vibration that strums
two tightly stretched membranes
amplified by the abdomen air chamber

there is a raw unified fire roaring
I become part of this unison
yet I have my distinctive song
a precarious balance
a knowing of individual essence and a loss of self
a death
an initiation
through an abyss of separation

some experiences root me to place
an artwork that both transcends its materiality
and communicates its form
music that has the spirit of the earth
language that lifts the head open

pieces of coal, black sound
the creation that climbs up inside you
the shadow inside is full of stardust and void and light
the art leads the hand curled around the shard of coal

kānuka

when kānuka grows collectively
they can look like rib bones, loose yet connected
their centres are hollowed out
spaces and cavities for spiders and wētā
as if marrow once flowed through

the lower kānuka branches break
they crack open a small wound
this grows over like a knuckle
a hollow knuckle, a knuckle to enter into
I enter in, a space dark
a space inside a space, nothing to hold onto

inside the marrow of kānuka
I move with the invisible weaver
I am inside an intelligent structure, a harmony of form
the sense of breath inside of bone

I sit under bony legs of tall straggly kānuka
in a sheltered hillside
clematis climbs into light
mingimingi, its soft dreamlike flowers fall over
droplets that race the air above a waterfall
pōhuehue finds its way through the grass
the edge of mown fields, twisting and stretching

I lean into the writing
I lean into communication
in the sand dunes the kānuka is the shelter
it leans into the wind, pushing out its arms
like a broken umbrella
limbs lean lanky

a blade of grass in the light
splinters the shadows

amongst a roiling wave of cicada chorus
I rest back on the ground
 and lose the thread I held loosely
within

6 fire

the grass is everyday

I see a bee
it is solitary

I am in a field
and the morning is late
the field is mid-summer
an old stone wall is crumbling
the grass is long, there are dandelions
wild carrot and plantain

I have run here from winter, the rush of time behind me
I forgot to stop in winter
and now in the summer in the warmth with a solitary bee
I remember

the hills around me
are dotted with sheep and erosion
sheep tracks pocket the curve of the hill
I think about pockets
and what they hide and carry and protect

time feels like a pressure
as if there are boundary lines around the space given
to this or to that

I am bound by time external
I sense the collective binding up of time
allocating time, tightening time

the night sets the dreamer free
to act and do
whilst it stands back a mute spectator

all this doing
the deceptive languid summer day is teeming, bustling
vibrant

the creation out of the dream
is as ephemeral as the dream

it is a curious phenomenon to see a bee solitary
when one bee is many bees
in its brain lives the hive

I get thrown over the wall
precipitous
to be thrown is a leap in the mind
there is no way to know how one gets from here to there
enough to know that the new here
has changed the way I perceive things

the presence of summer is like an unbounded child
I forget what is behind me and what is ahead of me

I leave the night behind

the ancestors are quiet

the grass is everyday
I look over it and from it
it is what we allow close up
I am amidst
silvery hair grass, fox tail, sweet vernal and wild oat
small white moths flutter up
daylight moths
delicate they merge with a whitening sky

beneath my feet
are generations of feet
our feet and grass
the dense, shallow fibrous roots of grass
roots threaded into each other, connecting and feeding

dandelion, plantaine, cleavers, yellow dock, wild carrot
carpet grass, cocksfoot, shivery grass and sweet vernal
in the sunlight, the longitudinal veins are standout ribs
that run parallel down the sheaf
exquisite light shimmers the shivery grass

in the summer my father cultivated
a diversity of grasses
by throwing the seeds

outwards
as if in memory of his ancestors
I remember the grasshoppers
and running through the long grass disturbing them
and the moths a rush of movement and life

Icarus with his feathers of constraint
forgot the way of equilibrium
and I too fly into the sun
but for the small cheeping of a sparrow

here is the everyday, the ordinary day, the people
the daily life

dandelion

in the meadow the cleavers
whirling growth barely perceived
the dandelion flowers are open to the sun
connected and present
upright and light

60

circle

like the grass and the bee I am part of a collective
my way forward is intimately connected with others
I cannot separate myself and think I am unrelated
my future is not a solitary line
intact as if a single I is the creator of it

the bees communicate how far away the nectar is
through a dance
there are two dances
the round dance and the waggling dance

I search for meaning
in amongst the grass
in amongst the cacophony of life

I look for the inherent pattern of things, the innate principle
I call to mind the branching patterns of rivulets of water
as they ribbon through the sand in the outgoing tide
how they look like a forest of trees

I connect through pattern
and the random miscellaneous company of plants

my hands lead me in a dance
first one hand then the other
my arms move and I open my body to the sun

pockets of darkness exude their sooty interior to the day
I form a circle with my arms
the shape of a continuous regular curve

there is strength in this gesture
I am reminded of the trunk of a tree
how it gives strength and structure
the sap moves, here is life force
and yet here is form defined

through gesture I can perceive through my body
experience different essences that exist within form
energies that have no form

I draw a circle in the ground

there is fluidity in inhabiting a circle

in drawing a circle
I divide the plane into two regions
an interior and an exterior, inner and outer
there is something complete
I am at a loss where to break into it
is this circle symbolic of the cyclical nature of existence
for I perceive it as unchanging, as perfect
where are the wisps of my undoing
the breaks and the disengagement
the parts I couldn't walk in my evolving cycle?

existence is forever changing

Aristotle considered time to be a circle
we live as if time is directional
a linear path that stretches between the past and the future
a desire to hold things in their imagined place, linearly

the light curves eventually back to itself

in this irreversible time
a death, a crumbling, a disintegration

time is paradoxical both circular and linear

everything within the circle exists outside of the circle
I step over the boundary
I stand inside the circle
I step outside the circle
there is a difference simply through the definition
to define the boundaries of existence

here in the late morning light
physical form is defined
colour exists within each form

it doesn't leak through the undifferentiated universe
my arms release the circle

codes and patterns

my hands form a cylinder with one fist over the other

the cylinder is a channel
perhaps more like a bridge that allows transition
between one space and another
one dimension and another

I stand in the diversity of the weeds
I can hear laughter
as I try to make secure
this new language of gesture

dandelion exists

I sense movement
that shifts into the temporal from somewhere other

dwarfs arrive
humorous and serious
light interfaces their being and doing
they stand in a line.
by putting one hand on their heads
and the other hand on their bellies
they form a backward S that is repeated like a wave

are they teasing me

as I clumsily edge my comprehension forward

gesture, symbol, idea
idea, symbol, gesture

the gesture lets in the idea

energy has movement
like a wave, it builds to an experience of intensity
reaching its peak it starts to move downwards
a release
there is another small build before it dissipates

the S shape is a wave, a sinusoidal wave
it is in my body, it begins in my heart

there are small electrical currents
that drive the beating of our heart
within the gesture of any one thing there is movement
in how we think and how we act there is movement
the wave allows for the continuity of movement
a movement of life force
rhythmic signals that pulse, build up, and release
energy in relationship to substance
substance in relationship to energy

through rhythm we join the dynamic relationship
between spirit and the physical world

I move my hand, drawing the infinity symbol
I allow my whole body to be led by my hand
I start from the left going towards the right
up and down the symbol of the wave
and then back and around

with this fluidity I no longer hold
onto what I might know
an imitation of the fluid transmutation of each thing

codes, patterns and rhythms
nature's leavings
they are interlacing filaments in a continuous web

in the interstices an aperture
the space allows the form

a single mark, a broken twig, a pebble, shape an association

they form texture
they become letters
the shape of the letter enfolds the pattern
they become words, resonate
evoking enduring images, memories and emotions

these patterns are remnants of rhythm
there in the markings of salt left in the sand
by the sea surging and moving through tides

the repetition gives it resonance
a line creates gesture

a line that looks like a bird's wing becomes flight
becomes movement in air, becomes the element of air
a hand that represents the wing of a bird
becomes intrinsically bound to us
we are in the weave, our wingless form knows flight

the dwarfs crowd around
each dwarf places his hands as a fist over each other
with elbows out on each side
they dance, creating formations that emanate outwards
I find myself embodying this dance
it is a synchronised movement
echoing a radiating creative universe
it re-jigs my inner patterns, patterns of thinking
patterns of survival, patterns through lineage

and then the dance pauses
I see a circle of four dwarfs in the centre
and eight surrounding them, forming an outer circle
there are lines of dwarfs radiating outwards
It reminds me of the organic chemistry formulas and
molecular structures from my father's chemistry books

I see the pattern as a matrix
moving from the inner recesses of our world
to the outer cosmos

place

the ground shook subtly
and every small dormant moth emerges
they flutter upwards from the grass
and the sky becomes soft in its embrace of them

I see their wings like small sculptured hands
as they merge into the pale light

I am reminded of being in Europe
in meadows alive with invertebrates
a landscape imprinted by the lives of people
a lineage where hunters and gatherers
assimilated to the forest
and people who settled in one place

there is a constancy of existence
that underlies the changing appearance of the world

this place, where I write, this small room in this valley
was once impenetrable forest
bursting with a cacophony of birds
a force of unmitigated creation lies under the grass

kākā

traversing the line between midnight and midday
kākā whistle eerily and then raucously call to each other
through the diurnal light
.

look at what we may hide from ourselves

in the midday, the kākā tears off the bark
it dips its beak, sharp into the wood
teasing out the pūriri moth larvae

the uncovering of truth, the ripping off the scab
secrets leak out joyous and blunt

the kākā is silent and solitary in the midday

and now the quiet
the quiet is a quiet that is searing
the quiet of a rose

I start looking for things to upset, to break the quiet
vulnerability, an awkward flower blooming

an oscillation springs up between love and loss
that causes my eyes to cast elsewhere
take your sight here, then there

a fly no longer buzzes in the desultory heat
but flies haphazard, hitting the window pane
even my phone is lighting up every three seconds
something falls off the bench in the corner

the kākā recognises the heart retreating
and bursting forth all at once
it tears the bark

I anchor
through touch

I attend

I reposition the objects that surround me
settling them in their positions
placement/tenderness/angles and patterns

attendance
through dedication

gold

there is a quivering of form
I have one leg through the floor

I move hampered
by the vision of floorboards
into a cavern
into a beneath world
inhabited by dwarfs

I am both in the earth and in my chest
I follow a spiral pathway down
there are dwarfs with pickaxes excavating gold

Rumpelstiltskin, a story from my childhood
would bring me to the edge of the chair
I related to the girl
who pretended she could spin straw into gold
an other-worldly gold from a room full of straw
a chimera, a fancy, a teller of tales
and the hard reality, the cold floor, a pile of straw
a spindle and a locked door

a little man arrives
yes he can spin straw into gold
an exchange happens between them
always the magical number three

with each telling of the story
I would have the same intensity of feeling
apprehension for losing what was important
her secrecy as an imposter
and the edges of two worlds meeting

I would paint the sun and the radiating rays
that pushed the edges of the page gold

in the cavern
the dwarfs show me the malleability of gold
mineral creativity
I excavate the gold of the dandelion flower
when it is open to the sun
there is a fleck and flutter of gold dust
the faces of the dwarfs turn gold, their sweat is gold
calendula flowers, golden rod, fields of wheat
pingao, the pollen on the bee
the copper of wētā, the iridescent wing
of the dragonfly reflecting sunlight
gold becomes ephemeral
unweighted dust spinning the straw into sky

the sun casts no shadow for me to find myself

I am a child
wearing sneakers
I free wheel, I run between crowds of people
show grounds, spectacles and markets
merry-go-rounds and Ferris wheels
everything is light, sunlight
summer crowds, cicada sound
the sun is bathing us in the heat
my feet become riveted to the ground
all around me is a unison of sound
the resonant song of cicada, falling and rifting

fragments slinter into a summer wave
pieces of me fall
through a sieve of light

I am

the wooden seats
weathering in the sun
the metal sheaths
in the wheel
old paint flaking into the grass

73

blackbirds scatter surface detritus
order hunts for reason

dedication
broken
falls from my hands piece by piece
I know no value

arrogance wants the emptiness to be recognised
as not empty

I become involved
rearranging the inside room
with unfitting pieces
the walls are flimsy

oh to be held
so that I may forget that I fell out of love with the beloved

soften, soften
in the quiet mist
in a drop of rain
on brittle stems

place these words upon the page
so things come into being

7 under the skin of the visible

in the bright light I cannot see stars. the impression is in the rock

the rock I pick up from the beach is powdery grey
although its edges are rounded, caressed by the sea
it appears chiselled
four sides angle towards a point from a square base
it is unassuming

I touch the fissures in the rock

the imprints and indents are like hieroglyphs
hewed by the sea

I place it in water on a small tidal island
in the predawn at the end of July
the tide is turning, the sky is clear
Matariki sparkles in the east

I get a glimpse of the capacity to stay open
and poised through fluctuations of emotions
shifts in character
the full and empty tide and changing seasons

the north spins the minerals through star dust
from the weavers in the southern night
I swim with shoals of fish
my body, ticklish with bubbles and lightness of touch

time has a long tail

I want to choose
yet I am in a place where there are no pathways
no decisions to make, no verdict in the rhythmic ocean
the hunt to choose diminishes, becomes indiscernible
until I am left with sweet attention

unbind by sensing the space and enter into it

I walk into merging edges
I imbibe the air
that settles amongst herbs and cottage plants
I see beauty in ordinary things, in cups of tea
in handmade cups, in rest and contemplation
ordinary things
ordinary events
time measuring change
washing dishes
looking through the window at the kererū in the nīkau
the feel of the cloth on the wooden bench
patterns in the wood, discarded objects
on the window sill, sweeping the floor
walking between rooms, between rooms

I listen to my pen marking the paper
as I write this word by word

I drop out of striving

in the intensity of light when I could not see
I did not pause
to wonder
purpose cut out the periphery

and now there is a dissolution of the questing
in the afternoon of reflection, I allow time to stretch out

pause
reflect
step forward
step back

shoes

the dwarfs are stitching
although their palms are large and their fingers short
they are nimble with their hands
they hold out a pair of shoes, leather shoes
shoes made individually for each foot
I am given leather shoe laces
I interlace them through finely stitched holes
I am reminded of the invention of things
we take for granted

when I place my feet into these shoes
how I think has a colour and a sensation
this makes me tentative as I walk forward

my feet act as antennae, visionary
in a sensate world

these shoes remind that I rarely lift out
of my perceiving
through the lens of history and culture
of my life and my parents lives

they reveal how everything within the landscape
encounters me or my absence
my feet interlace with the rich layered cognisance of earth

a blackbird turns its dark eye to look brightly
it flies up, perches on a low branch of the apple tree
the tree is in winter, the branch stark
it accentuates the separations and the spaces
I watch inside myself where I have turned away
the apple tree is old and worn by cicada

sparrows settle on the branches with a whirr of wings
waiting to catch a few grains from the wheat
that I feed the chickens
the blackbird nonchalantly hops back to earth
scratching in the leaf litter
I look down at my feet

the sleeping soul cannot hear the messenger

I regard the involute belief that assumes a lack of time
a sense of urgency pushes me to rush over what is beneath my feet
underneath the appearance of doing
a deep resistance, a turning away

I disrupt the inter-dreaming life
here is the sleep life, the slow drag, the careful closing of space
my landscape fills with the measure of time

the inner starts to bang pots and pans and shout incoherently

wētā presses its long antennae through the cracks of the wood
in slow motion fluid feeling, it senses how space is
old sunlight in darkness
movement that was disjointed
is now poised between the breaths of linear time
a creaking nudging antennae
alight on a sleeping hand, a hand given over to the cotton mill
its descendant hands stills sleep in the frayed contracts

a memory of warmth held frozen in time
stirs in the light probing from the wētā's antennae

a stiff crackling of awakening

before I know where I am, I am in darkness

a darkness between the crisscross of twigs and branches
in the mounds of earth that build slow and damp under bark
the smell of fungi sprouting early unseen amid the fecundity

darkness that is complete and timeless
darkness that renders stillness to the visitor that I am
darkness that rasps up against the memory of creation

I shift the weight of my feet, rocking towards a different alignment
to the click-click of wētā
and the continual damp intelligence of earth and water

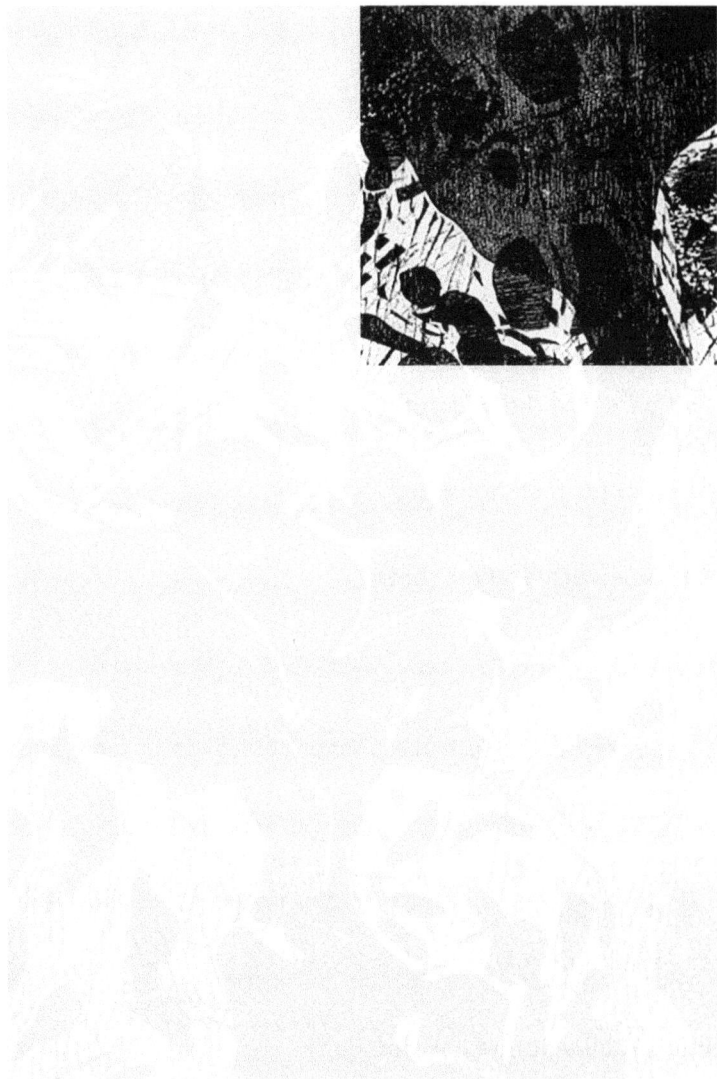

8 moon

silver

an ethereal light
plays
with shadowed form

a hand cautiously comes into sight
I follow its indistinct outline
and perceive the body of a man lying on his side
a giant
his vast form shimmering

he plays with a silver thread
exquisite
in its movement
it tantalises, pulses
its tattered end glints like phosphorescence in wet sand

there is an invitation
to let go the doing, the planning,
touch the mysterious
alive and unknown

buoyed by a gentle current
I float above a sleeping landscape

before dropping
steadily to the ground

the man in the moon

snow wafts down burying sound, it lies in deep drifts
shrouding

the fir forest
I shelter into the broken twigs

with inexorable movement the giant rises
trees bend and crack
resounding through the muffled landscape

he picks me up, friendly and curious

there is no purpose in his walk, there is no need or demand
he walks silvery light

I look down upon moonlit landscapes, dangling in his hand

he puts me down
in a startling barren landscape
a place both true and not true

contrasts merge
into shadow ghosts
a monotonal play in an unreal light

I am with the man in the moon

my senses take as a known factor our gravitational weight
without this
I look for my body behind me
I remember rock
which I touch before my fingers can land on it

sound is starlight crackling

I am surrounded by absence
the memory of familiar objects
become dry sketches
in an oscillating fabric

the pattern of things is broken by their omission

everything that was, is no longer
and everything that is, is no longer what it seems
what moment of choice
what moment of desire swept me here?

bare
words stark in the silver light

children's rhymes
nonsense poems
Jonathan Jo has a mouth like an O
and a wheelbarrow full of surprises

reflection

I become aware of appearances
I want to
see in a mirror

I stretch out
lethargic and large
I feel too big for the moon
the moon undulates in liquid light

I fall off the moon and become suspended in nothing
a wind comes from below

with unhurried grace, I float down
my legs stretch, my feet bump into the earth

I stand on a narrow bank of sand edging an estuary
what is left of the moon are blurred lines of light
and shadow across the wavering surface of water
the tide begins to ebb
the current fluctuates, stretches
and then a quiet rush to the mouth of the estuary
the surface is a skin of shimmering fish scales

the ebb surges inwards
in my blood

the ocean
the tide
the moon

the moon tugs
the earth accommodates, the water pulls back
breath breaks open the tiny bivalves
lifeforce swells and eddies

in the estuary the currents are swift and sometimes hidden
the wind ruffles the surface
I watch the agitation
I watch the settled times
the changing colours as the mud flats are revealed
I think how I might allow my life force to be lost
forgetting to attend to its natural rhythm
I might give it away or allow it to be stolen

in the sand dunes Californian lupin
unmoored yellow blossoms

the lupin has a sweet taste
the light yellow edge of its colour splashes
into spaces that open around my clavicle
I swallow

a seeping light like a liquid jewel
trickles into shadow places

leaking into inflexible partitions
where criticism has lingered
and stricture builds a wall with whatever material
is available

though indistinct boundaries
I become a geometry
fitted together

I journey and do not move

the land is the galaxy within my body
I am a shimmery outline
I reach out for reference points
I am this, you are that
I am human, you are land

the moon blends its light with morning

wētā shyly moves inexorably into the west
sparrows gather, cheeping noisily

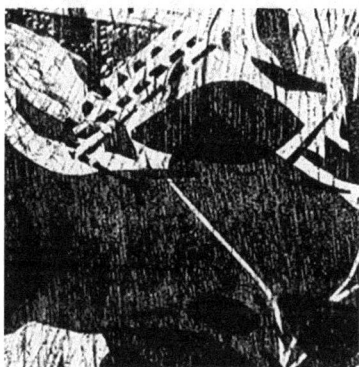

9 water

river

nephrite through movement
and collision
along a plate boundary
is pushed to the surface of the earth

the river sooths its fire
liberates pounamu
is faithful to its rough surface

pounamu

a stir of viridescent flight
flecks, inclusions, distinct compositions of green
and slivers of white
great sorrow, tumultuous joy
river caught in stone

essence of matter
is movement

and the river is clear
fast flowing
tumbling
rippling back

eddies
and softens

uncovers rich brocades
ribs of calcite in concretion
furrowed schist

tiny cascade flies
frail counterpoints to the rush of water
fly up to capture miniature flying insects
which they lacerate with saw edged jaws
near invisible the pupae cling to the stones
with clusters of gills and circular suckers

the water
spins pebbles
until they settle into banks of fit-in-a-child's-palm stones
forming cell-like patterns
as they bump into each other

sandfly larvae hook into submerged stones
through a gelatinous substance
secreted by its saliva glands
they stand leaning with the current
tiny mouths with hairy brushes trail in the passing water

the river surges, smooth stones pile up behind boulders
a slap and rush of sound that clears the mind
near the banks water oscillates
forms miniature streams
and sandy islands

memories eddy and hang here, lipping subtle sounds
so one presses one's ear in the shallow waters
into
the edge places and the babbling soft reeds

every nuance washes up debris
collecting in and around shafts of memory
like the way the light slants back
through from the west

interior

I walk beside the river
picking my way around ferns
arrested by the flickering reflections
on the surface of the water
I enter into an interior world of emotions

a blade of fear, the fragile tongue of resentment
the shadow wing of revenge
arrogance, hasty and sharp entangles the light
guilt travels with fragmented memory
and the shards of unfinished business

I observe with relentless scrutiny
unattended relationships, unfulfilled expectations
and the unstated expectation
that can only be read with an invisible cultural handbook

I crave to blanket sensitivity
any which how

the past becomes hidden amongst memory
I am chased by splinters of loneliness
fragments of un-belonging join with poignant shadows
that forget they are formed from the sun

the threshold in the west accents my separation

a trickle of stories helps me find my way
little Vasalisa found her allies through small attendances
in the shadow of Baba Yaga

forest stories finger my senses
the alone journey, magical meetings
sharing the final crust of bread to a small bird
the sun in winter
a quest initiated and fulfilled through an innocent heart

every river has its essence
this one rushes forth from a lake
I kneel down by the edge and let my fingers trail through
its vibrant surface
in this gesture I offer something of myself
and yet it is not clear to me what it is

it is what is underneath my thoughts and insecurities
that meets and is met by river

west

the day softens its edges into darkness
a chatter of birds
the internal bright day given voice

the shadows in the forest grow thick
the rich layered sound of song birds drops away
I am left with the bell tenors of a tūī
ending with a rich chortle and the rhythm of river

there, in the shadows is a house
unlike the stories, I hold fast to my aloneness
I resist the desire to open the door
inattention to the action that beckons
is to linger in restriction and constraint at the threshold

my soul is waking up the door
it stands leaning towards it
my soul cannot open the door without me
I look away

water has eroded the soil away from the tree roots
they form wide dresses
that hang with lacing and twisted roots

I worry about how I got here
what could I have done differently in the past
I look so hard that my eyes hurt

the plant scrambling fumitory weaves along and upright
its translucent crimson flowers poke out like tongues
it has been named smoke of the earth by Piny the Elder
for when your eyes are rubbed by it
it brings tears like encountering acrid smoke

the plant acts as sentinel
is an indicator for what is present here
lenses tilt perspective
I rub my eyes

rain falls into the top canopy of the trees
it drips slowly
down
water runs into the landing place for my souls tears
I hold tight, vigilant
I stare beyond the river and the trees
dissecting my past

until the ancestors rush
through me
without knowing
what I am doing
I have joined my soul at the doorway

I push open the door
my soul rejoices

this house is not a house
it is atrium
its pillars hold up nothing but the sky
I falter
nothing is what I expect it to be
I cannot know what is true
from forming an idea from the past

a sparrow flies through the frame of sky
and enters a crowd of cheeping

I walk through
into a bustle of people preparing food
lighting a fire

come
into
the night

we eat and talk
and the night is touched
by our flickering flames
and the sound of the river rushing

mosquito

the larvae and pupae of the mosquito
inhabit the standing and sluggish water
where water pools and settles under leaves
in the nīkau fronds, in small indents
in boles and the boughs of trees

there is a single objective in the female mosquito
the search of blood
she lands on birds and mammals
she inserts her proboscis

the mouth of the mosquito looks like a tiny spear
yet under a microscope
there are six needle like mouth parts
each of these pierces the skin

this single mindedness disrupts my own
it disturbs my sleep
the native vigilant mosquito whines at night
whilst the little tiger striped mosquito
is silent in its hunt

I begin my life dependent, in the raiment of frailty
and resilience, I grow into my unfinished states

I let the mosquito, land on my arm

I watch her probe my skin

she finds the blood vessel

her tiny body pulses with my blood

in this small surrender

I hardly feel her light body or her taking of my blood

lake

in the breeze, newly hatched spiders go ballooning
catching the air currents on threads of silk
I see fragments as the sun glints upon them
thousands of fine threads of silk
attached to tiny spiders floating through the air
graceful, airborne, sallying forth into the unknown
letting go

to let go
is to allow someone or something to escape
to relinquish one's grip

I think of a young child gripping a ball
unable yet to know how to release it
and the beauty of that joyful act
when finally the ball is let go of
perhaps it is something to practice
a daily letting go, a daily unfurling

a burden might gather weight
become habitual
through ancestral memory
knotted fragments of other lives
held like an anchor when the wind blows
 the thistle seeds
high in the autumn sky

letting go occurs when I am not watching
in a rhapsodic moment I forgot what I was holding
it escaped unbeknownst

I become aware of its weight due to its absence

now it is gone

the burden built a purpose
now without it life becomes ill-defined

day and night slip from one to the other

I sit on the shore of a lake
I watch the reflection of the moon in the water
its ravaged face rippling

the moon has an orbit, one side always in darkness
it seems that looking now requires blindness
there is nothing but to open up
and stretch into emptiness

I ease into a quietude
the lake rolls and lushes with the stones

ocean

the ocean reflects the rhythm of the cosmos
again and again
it slips me in
dreaming, lulled by the wash of waves
deep timeless drifts
currents
no craft

chambered nautilus

a chambered nautilus moves shell first, buoyant
oscillating backwards, fluid in its movement
luminous in its form
it ascends to the surface to feed
its tentacles smelling and manipulating
moving and trailing in the ocean behind it

the curvature of its shell
translucent and delicate,
follows a logarithmic spiral
with each turn being exactly three times the size
of the one before it
its shape is unaltered with each successive curve

somehow
from tiny soft folds of convoluted tissue
the nautilus constructs its shell
as soon as it's hatched from the egg

beginning like a small seed, pea sized, it grows
by each successive stage of its development
it moves into a new chamber
and seals off the old chamber
these chambers are gas filled flotation chambers
each chamber is connected by a small tube
which acts like a siphon

regulating the density of gas
enabling the nautilus to rise to the surface of the water

its essence appears in the oscillating movement
a movement emanating from essential form
immersing in depth with lightness

from a place of immersion
in the secret substrata and recesses of matter
form envelopes space, gives voice to space.

blind to where it is leading
we evolve through a narrative
that exists through the act of living
within this unravelling living scroll
I have an access to totality
and sudden flashes of inspiration that shift swiftly
from one state to another

I am a child, an adult, an old person
in the ocean everything exists at once
a layering of time, time folding back over

to exist here is to rest in rhythm
I am in the lilt and the release
I am in a medley of all my encounters
connections that led me forward, connections
discarded, connections that held me captive

thieves, bullies, martyrs, desirous and revengeful

the chambered nautilus moves backwards
to the surface
where the light penetrates the water
looking backwards entering light

huia

I walk through ocean
until I hear a reverberation in my heart
until I sense the wind comes to
until I smell curling smoke from a fire
until I meet
huia

I begin my sentence in one century and end it in another

I walk under huia and the tōtara tree
standing in distant gateways
I enter reverence
whilst being unpracticed in listening
I fold up my broken cloth
my ancestors had given me
to keep it orderly

I fold up
the witness
I lean down on the creases of wisdom and despair

I watch the me that surrenders
to the male huia
that puts his beak in my throat

opening the way for the female huia
to pull forward sweet maggots of decay

10 to shape

making

I am told, through stories
that the dwarfs do not serve the will of a person

the dwarfs make beautiful things for the gods
they make mead for wisdom
and they have a love of gold

there is power in making things
an invitation for love
the basket we weave in the sun by the flax
the clay we use, the cups we drink out of
a memory where earth is met
and mingled with the spirit
leaping sudden and complete

the dwarfs will support one to redress the balance
caused through greed and material hording
they test your generosity
and how well you understand
the spirit of life force in relationship to creativity
and the material world
three times they will appear
each time an offering is accepted

if the dwarfs are forced to create something through
magic

or through the power of will
then they will weave a dark spell into the very things
they are forced to create

it is uncomfortable to serve the will of others
to continue to override
the one inside that desires its voice
the soul will sleep and only emerge
when my hands find their service

the old woman takes my hands
and sees in the creases and the whorls
what has governed me and who I serve
I have to find the old ones
that live in the torn away lands
the forgotten dimensions under the dawn
I serve these ones

only then can I change the pathways
embedded like riverbeds in my palm

karamū

a small field of honeysuckle
each summer the sound of bees
the sweet smell of nectar
creamy white flowers
light green leaves that bind over themselves

karamū, Coprosma robusta, a small shrub
grows through the honeysuckle
that binds down its branches

yet karamū grows sturdy and vital
irrepressible it has mettle and pluck

I crawl through the honeysuckle
and lie inside it looking up into karamū
at the creamy white filaments of its flowers
and orange berries
I see branches that are dead and branches finding leaf
pushing through
sparking

11 mountain

elements

when I close my eyes I see a sleeping hound
when I notice it
it stands up
licks my ear and settles down on my left side
it becomes a companion as I walk
I know that it will come and go

I enter a forest
where light shimmers through the understory
there are bright blue toadstools
and tiny white filaments
branching out of the decaying wood

the light unexpectantly picks out
the dark ovoid shell back of a cockroach
as it slips into the debris of the forest floor
disappearing from sight
I step over large branch-like roots
I climb over fallen trunks and buttresses

I am reminded of a story
where dwarfs emerged from the maggots
that eat a giant buried in the earth
decay cleaning the dead, transformed into life

I walk along the edge of an open hill
small shimmers of clouds drift up
ghostly breaths

whip-chord hebe and heather intermingle with tussock
eaten back by hares
the wind and the winter's snow have folded
their hand upon the stiff branches of Dracophyllum
leaving their skeletal structures upright
bone grey

clouds shift and roil across the sky
creating bands of light and shadow
rain arrives and departs
water darts and cascades in intimate play with rock
all the small existences laid bare
the hills marked with erosion
in the distance sparse dots of stone and lichen
are interspersed with red tussock

flowers so subtle I might miss them

the inflorescences of the beech are small
in the axils of the uppermost bud scales of new shoots
these are the male flowers
the female flowers are in the axils
of lowermost new leaves on the same tree

the mountain Astelia grow beside the stream
Astelia nervosa, Astelia without a stem

miniature streams pool over fallen debris
sometimes clear, other times dark and boggy
tiny sundews grow
crimson red with star like protrusions
native daphne, hebe, mountain tutu, mānuka
a chaffinch sits in the toatoa chirruping

hare

I become hare

preening

taking care to attend to small ticks or fleas

I have a hunger that is keen

as I am bound forward

the landscape bounds through me

falcon man

on an outcropping of rock
looking out
over the herb fields
stands a magical being

he has distinctive markings on his face
the sharp lines delineate the structure of his head
that is half bird and half human
he has a curved beak, his eyes are large and fierce
there are light feathers at his throat

there is a particularity in how I see him
and the landscape around him
small details are accentuated
the rock, the orange of the lichen
cradled in mist and the closely hanging cloud

the falcon man has a crest on his forehead
I see the blackness of his eyes
I am reminded of a seer
I see sky in him, balance in him

there are feather tuffs on his head
his eyebrows are protruded
he is both feminine and masculine
his pronoun is he

he is a hunter, if he had a bow and arrow
the arrow would be poised directly at me

I am mesmerised, held still by this

it is pivotal to the hunter, attention to detail
and a consistent awareness
of the interrelated landscape

everything is of significance, the small and the large
it is meaningful who I have been in the past

the look I am withstanding is the anthesis of indulgence
I am shown a way of action
through connection to the whole landscape
an implacable trust in existence
a quality of strength
that is gained through heightened sensitivity

when I lose connection
when I forget that my everyday survival
is in relationship with nature
then I lose humility

humility is the aligned position
from the finite to the infinite
from the part to the whole

attendance to the small
creates harmony
creates balance

in looking into the falcon man's eyes
I am aware of my dependence
on that which is greater than myself
and a fluid interdependence with people

his gaze penetrates my fragility until I arrive at dignity

he eats a grasshopper
with fierce attendance

transition

I walk through the dense herb fields
where *Dracophyllum*, hebes and native daphne
are interspersed with bog pine and mountain toatoa
I watch where I place my feet
as the ground can drop suddenly into deep ruts
elements are exposed, red clay, black bog, rock
wind deer eat at the exposed ash hills that erode in
great curves
beech forest strays a little up the mountain

12 earth

tree

I arrive into a small gathering of mountain beech
spindly trunks marked with silver lines

moss finds anchor in a large battered beech tree
its branches twist and open an umbrella of twigs
to the storms

through a circuitous entry
I find a soft hiding place
within the recess of bole and trunk
I rest

I lay down
in old arms
hidden and gruff

resounding quiet

time becomes adrift

when I move
I create noise
a crinkling, a rustling
the tree has roots that river deep into the earth
I am a tickle on the surface

my feet
touch down
on soft layers of small leaves
that petal the mossy ground

in the beech forest

as I look at the spindly delicate trunks my vision wavers
the dying light plays upon the silver lines
that mark the bark
like a quivering flame

amongst the roots a movement, snake-like
darkness opens its jaw
I step in
spiralling
through blankets of earth

surrounding me
a continuous pulsing
a rhythmic beating

a darkness like breath
empty then full, meets and disappears

I trust the interface that my feet have with earth
a reminder of the distinction of form
for darkness allows form to become adrift

my feet and rock notice each other
curious of how each exists
rock introduces crumbling

sediment

consolidation

water

smooth

sharp

my feet tentative

confident

and then a slow resistance

as if, as if

I touch my feet

reminding me of belonging

be longing

I belong

I tell my fingers

as I move through earth

dimensions and space coalescing

a synthesis of earth and air

hidden

I am
walking/resting/falling
the unfathomable

through
both the dream mountain
and the mountain that exists in its physical form
I traverse through rock
suspended in the mystical element of rock

geological millennia
imprinted in petrified whorls and waves
stillness of death transcribed and cast as incorruptible
fragments where once sap ran

time elapses
unexplored

and future is indelibly marked
into the interior of stone

memory
transposes to visions
place themselves on the periphery of thought

I am in the

breaking down

in layers

in stone stories

of transient life that rises

from oblivion

diamond

I see dwarfs mining the interior of minerals
cracking open stones to reveal the harmony of geometry
the correspondence of patterns
likeness and difference within the span of our minds

sometimes a stone holds a drop of water
for millions of years

diamond
a volatile creation
pushed up through magma from the earth's mantle

clarity, unbreakable

I carry a small diamond in a glass of water through rain
water pools and trickles through the subcanopy
I raise the glass and let these sparkling ephemeral drops
run down the inside of the glass

exposing a world reflected in a drop of water
a fragile transient existence
before it melds with the water in the glass

the emperor allowed the nightingale
the freedom to exist
vulnerability through love

when I write soul

when I write soul
I write earth
the physicality of form
and the mystical aspects that are conjoined into it
I imagine sinuous folds and sudden spaces
wind singing and the singe of fire on skin

13 soul

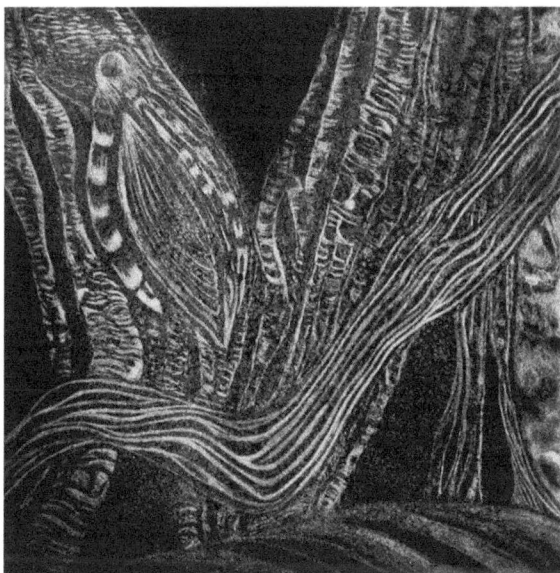

taurepo

I enter through a filament
a hair of a root through a fissure in rock

I emerge through water seeping into a narrow crevice
with clay cliffs embedded into the greywacke rock

taurepo, *Rhabdothamus solandri*
grows slowly close to the ground
branching out into small shrubs on the cliffs
it has striking orange flowers that hang like small bells
delicate in the midst of its orbicular leaves
It grows in the understory
and gives the impression of spaciousness

it is a late comer in the evolution of plants in Aotearoa
and is fertilised by the oldest honey eater the hihi
who flits through the understory of the forest

holding to the edge of the cliff with taurepo
I catch a glimpse of other realms of existence
I discover softening, an ability to settle
in places uncomfortale
I find I am able to enter into a surrendered state of being
observe without gripping onto meaning
nor desire to possess what is always transient

the door left open

I dream of a young man
who grows up in a small protected religious sect
he is loved and I am related to him
and so I can visit him

as I open the door something wild follows me in
there is havoc in the stone walls
a jarring
I have disturbed the peace in the world within the
room
in that protected room I discover myself
a wild fluttering
that makes me afraid

I take his young hand
I hold it gently
and feel a contradiction of a desire to open and con-
tract

we leave what has kept us safe

I cannot shut down love
I cannot shut down the sense of vulnerability
for the soul exists and evolves
in the state of this fragility of being

moss

through the light rain on moss there is starlight
a sharp bright light and the softness of moss
I imagine moss
when I have to slowly touch the cracking
open of my wild skin

moss brings with it
a memory of walking through wet forest
the trickle of rain dripping through leaves
sweet tears of water that takes space in my body
like an internal babbling brook
filtering through into stagnant places
empty of touch

playful immediacy
impermanent gardens
home

fragments

I take plantain into the palm of my hand
the veins
enter into my hand
these veins are ribs
pathways that converge and open up
into internal spaciousness

my posture becomes upright,
it is the posture that propels me forward

I fall
I see flashes of effigies of an ancient mother
clay objects discarded
images of tenderness
hands that caress
remains of woven cloth
unravelling threads of light

I fall slowly
through an earth that remembers separation
through the neglect to find the language of stone
and the desire to cut away from vulnerability

I fall through unspoken voices
that could not find the untraceable stories
and the stones that buried their grief

I float through frozen worlds
where all is in a state of suspension
I see effigies burning
with quick fiery fervour, a desire to destroy
something old
some old woman

because of the difficulty of her demands upon her children

I see her enter the darkness
through cities of lost people
I lose sight of her
I am in slow stagnant spaces of despair
where time is left to roam
I imbibe and spit out the disdain
that people have for the ordinary and the abundant

in a constant state of fragmentation
my tattered wings
become soft powdery moth wings
beating the thick night

do not lose this
piece of soul

do not
deprive the world of meaning

I walk

I walk
amongst crickets
a tinny orchestra of song before summer appears

I walk
a path strewn with the tiny exoskeletons of insects
I walk upon their shells
my feet bare in supplication
each step to admit the existence of these tiny shells that
have come to life and death like waves
to acknowledge surges of life on a vast scale
to engender balance

I walk
into Hekate
through her mouth of worms
the debris of decaying leaves
glutinous golden secretion of algae, wet fungi

I walk
through discarded bones
the mineral trickling breakdown

I walk
loneliness
I walk the loss of self in walking the unwalkable

I walk
until grief is empty

I walk
clouds of fawn coloured moths
spiral out from the ground and the surrounding trees
the breath of Hekate

I walk into breath

praying mantis, mystical and separate
exudes its eggs, creamy brown caskets in dry crevices

large dragonflies land on my arms
ancient eyes and old wings
latticing light forming a rainbow sheen
before they lift off with awkward grace

black and coppery cockroaches crawl across the ground
a flicker of gold in the wet sheen of their shields

a thread is pulled
creating a gathering of hidden crevices
earth folds
into the heart of Hekate

unmoored from my body
language decomposes

let be

she creates silences around things
I meet myself

teeming with insects

go with the hound

I go with the hound
there is no path
the hound is courage, instinct and loyalty

through ravaged landscape
scrubby margins of pasture, wasteland
solanum linnaenum or the apple of Sodom growing
haphazardly, spiny, branching in all directions
small yellow and green apples

I run
the hound on my left side
past pools of stagnant water
unattended pockets of sadness
mouldering rooms
neglected cloakrooms
empty clothes
stations of waiting
souls who forget their existence

I go through the place of sleeping beings
unable to wake
they drape over the boughs of mahoe and hangehange

I want to lie down and rest and lose my way
settle with moonlit dreams

the hound nudges me forward

a slow sluggish passage
blindness
edges up my legs
it seeps into my bones

I hold the neck of the hound
I cannot go on, I want to sleep for a long time
the hound pushes me through a wall
I daren't look back

and if I go down the branches

I step into a room
in the room is a fire
an open fire with a black kettle

as I see it, it disappears

I am without reference point
I am without energy and desire

I am aware of stars shimmering
pearls drawn on a wall

the darkness folds away from me
as I remember stories and ancestral relationships
the tree grows
its roots spread up, its branches move down

I climb into the underworld
I follow a root
it is a very ordinary root
I am grateful for its
instinctive resilience

it takes up residence

the root imbibes the moon
until it becomes a luminous thread
that I hold between my forefinger and thumb

I hear
tiny bumping sounds like grain trickling
I smell the scent of sediment
separated from the ocean
I taste the empty oyster shell
washed up

Hekate

Hecate is here
in the places between the roots
she weaves a remembering
of the space between the threads

she passes it through shadows and across thresholds
through death and into our grief
she brings it through our life force

my soul evolves through the narrow openings
through cracking and the splitting
through a lemniscate of crossing pathways

I hold my hands over my eyes

light traces

the dying pūriri moth
fluttering
a spilling of soft powder before
the dawn edges its light and the
ruru darts silently down

I open my hands

inside
out

Acknowledgements

Thank you to Meggan Young for your love and support and also helping me purchase and install my little fireplace in my studio. It kept me warm in the early hours of the morning as I hand wrote the first drafts by candlelight during the months of May, June, and July in 2019. The writing of this work continued for over five years. Thank you to Mike Johnson, for your faith in me and for the deep slow read, as we tested the sound of my words and meaning. I am grateful to this small valley I live in and the challenging experience of writing in the presence of other-worldly beings and elementals. To Daniela Gast and Rowan Sylva, thank you for all the work you do for Lasavia Publishing and bringing this book to fruition.